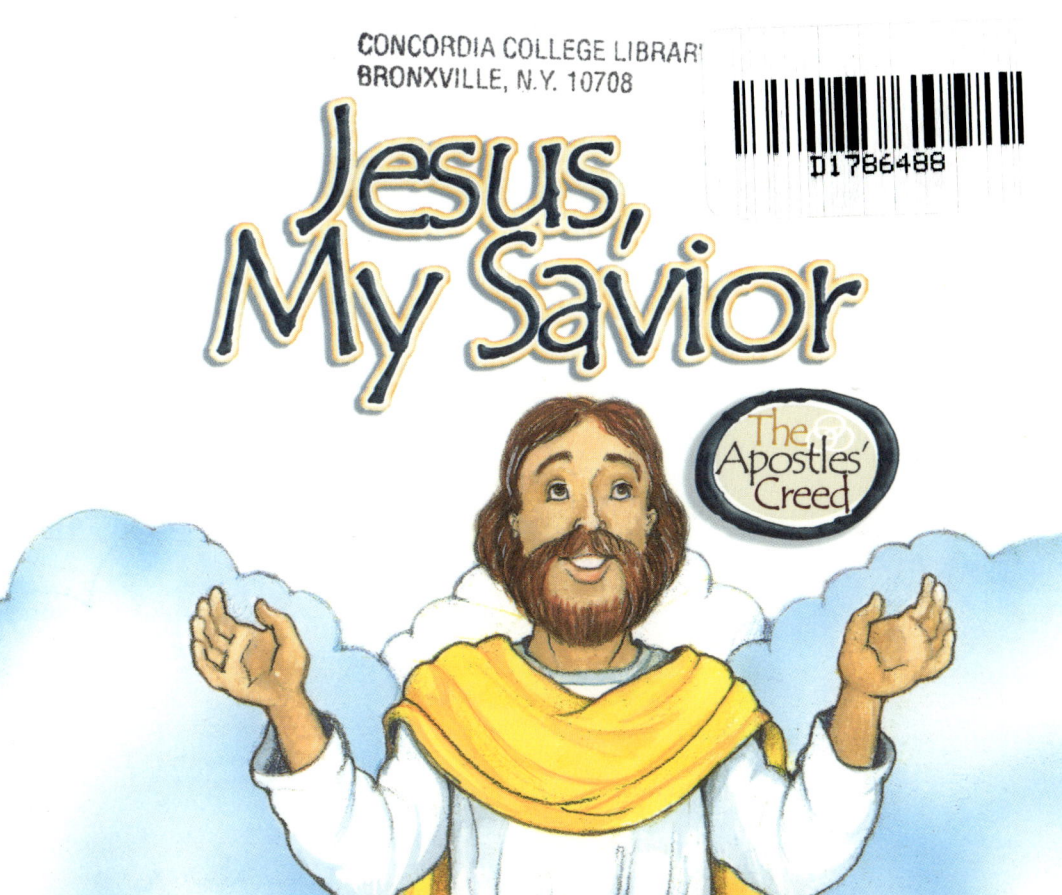

Jesus, My Savior

The Apostles' Creed

The Book of Luke and Acts 1 for children

Written by Jim Gimbel and Abby Gimbel
Illustrated by Susan Morris

Arch® Books
Copyright © 2003 Concordia Publishing House
3558 S. Jefferson Avenue, St. Louis, MO 63118-3968
Explanation to the Second Article of the Apostles' Creed taken from
Luther's Small Catechism with Explanation. Copyright © 1986 by Concordia Publishing House.
Manufactured in Colombia
All rights reserved. No part of this publication may be reproduced, stored in a retrieval system,
or transmitted, in any form or by any means, electronic, mechanical, photocopying, recording,
or otherwise, without the prior written permission of Concordia Publishing House.

The boys on the seashore were learning their trade.
They worked hard, they listened, and sometimes they played.
They were taught how to sail, clean a fish, mend a net.
They learned all day long from sunrise to sunset.

Their master was Clement, who had learned at this shore
From a fisher named Peter, who knew fish and more.
He taught all that he knew; fishing secrets he shared,
But he also taught Jesus, with whom none compared.

As the boys cleaned the fish and their chatter would run,
Clement told the great deeds of Jesus, God's Son,
Who was promised to Eve, to Abram and Ruth,
To all who would listen and hear of God's truth.

How God's Son, humbly born, though the King of creation,
Was the Savior of all, including God's nation;
Born of a virgin, sweet Mary, by name;
Pledged to Joseph, to whom angel Gabriel came.

With God His true Father and Mary His mother,
Full God and full man has no equal, no other.
He was human completely, but yet without sin.
He had all the God-powers, full of grace from within.

"Was He spirit alone in a body we see?"
"Was He just a great man God adopted, like me?"
"Did He switch between God and the man as He chose?"
"No, no, no," said Clement, like a teacher who knows.

Then the girl with a jar said, "I don't understand.
Is Jesus true God, or is Jesus true man?"
Said Clement, "He's both, in a way we can't see.
As true God, He forgives all; as true man, dies for me."

"So tell us some stories," the boys begged for more.
"Well," said Clement, "He once taught from this very shore.
He healed many, like lepers, fed folks fish and bread;
He calmed a great storm, water-walked, raised the dead.

"But of all the great things in His life that He did,
The best deed of all? When He died for us, kid!
Though He never did sin or commit any crime,
He was captured and tried before Pilate one time.

"He was hung on a cross, where He suffered and died,
While His followers watched from a distance and cried.
His body was buried in a borrowed new tomb;
His full person, dead briefly, was not held in gloom.

"He announced throughout hell that a victory He'd won;
He didn't stay dead; by His life, Life's begun!
When He rose from the dead three days after the grave,
He revealed to believers His power to save.

"The good news for us, my dear friends, as you see,
  Is that through Jesus' death, He's redeemed you and me.
  Although we are lost and condemned by our sin,
  By Christ's death on the cross, resurrection WE win!

"He buys us all back, as the Scriptures have told,
  But with His lifeblood, most precious, not silver or gold.
  Since the wages of sin have been taken away,
  We now can be with Him forever some day.

"Forty days after He rose from the dead,
  He went back to heaven, just as He said.
  He sits by the Father on a great and high throne
  Where He rules and He reigns and His name is well-known.

"From there He'll come back, though we do not know when.
But He'll judge every person who's ever lived, then.
And all who believe He's the Truth, Life, and Way—
Their Redeemer and Savior—with Him they will stay.

"Now since we know that we are His own,
We don't need to fear; we are never alone.
He's defeated the devil; He's conquered our sin.
Through His resurrection, even death cannot win."

The boys learned of Jesus from Clement each day.
They lived for, served, loved Him, and often did say,
"I believe in this Jesus, my God who's the Word,
He's most certainly, truly, my Savior and Lord."

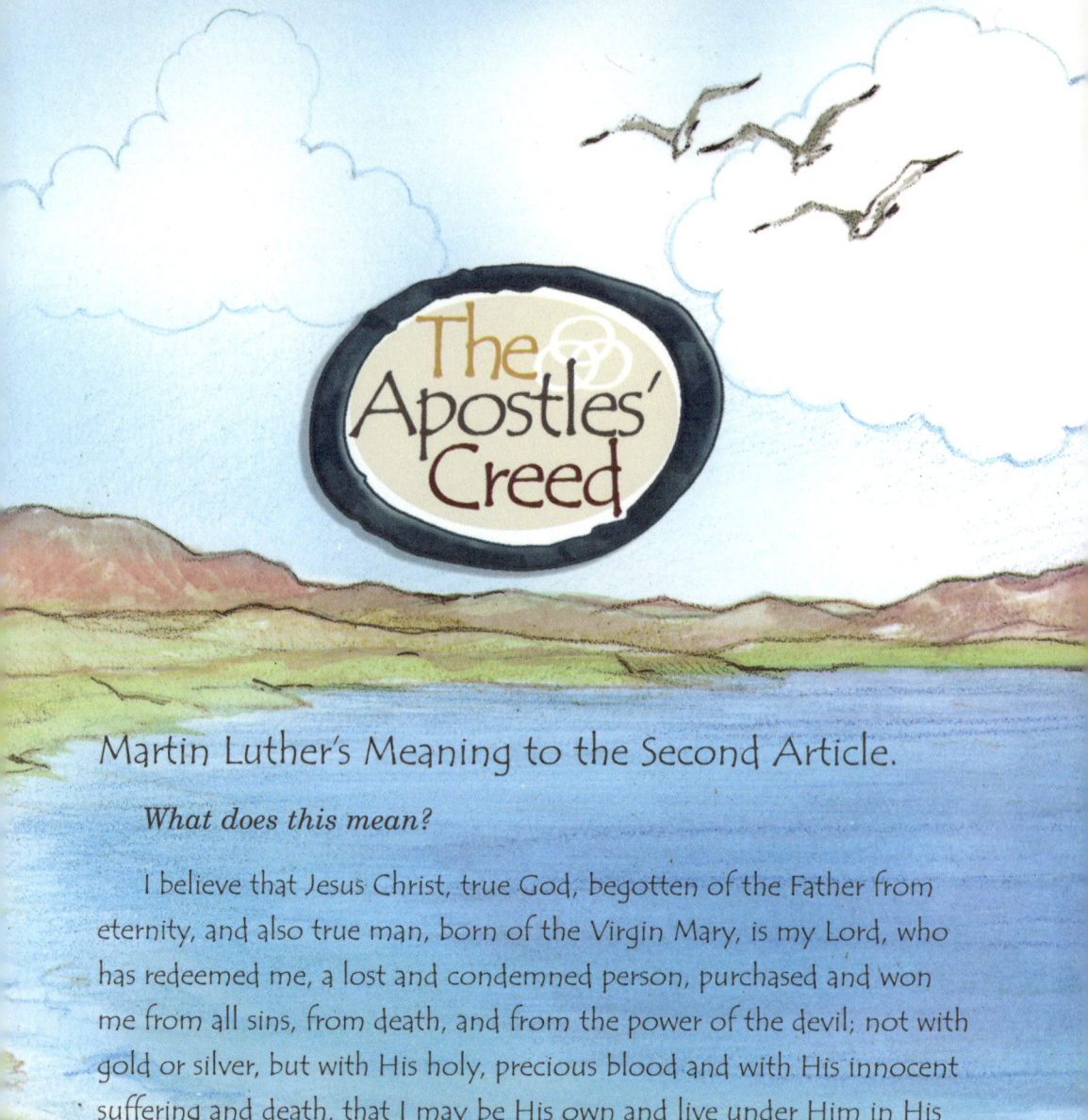

The Apostles' Creed

Martin Luther's Meaning to the Second Article.

What does this mean?

I believe that Jesus Christ, true God, begotten of the Father from eternity, and also true man, born of the Virgin Mary, is my Lord, who has redeemed me, a lost and condemned person, purchased and won me from all sins, from death, and from the power of the devil; not with gold or silver, but with His holy, precious blood and with His innocent suffering and death, that I may be His own and live under Him in His kingdom and serve Him in everlasting righteousness, innocence, and blessedness, just as He is risen from the dead, lives and reigns to all eternity. This is most certainly true.

I believe in God, the Father
Almighty, Maker of heaven and earth.

And in Jesus Christ, His only Son, our Lord,
who was conceived by the Holy Spirit,
born of the Virgin Mary,
suffered under Pontius Pilate,
was crucified, died and was buried.
He descended into hell.
The third day He rose again from the dead.
He ascended into heaven
and sits at the right hand of God,
the Father Almighty.
From thence He will come to judge
the living and the dead.

I believe in the Holy Spirit,
the holy Christian church,
the communion of saints,
the forgiveness of sins,
the resurrection of the body,
and the life everlasting. Amen.

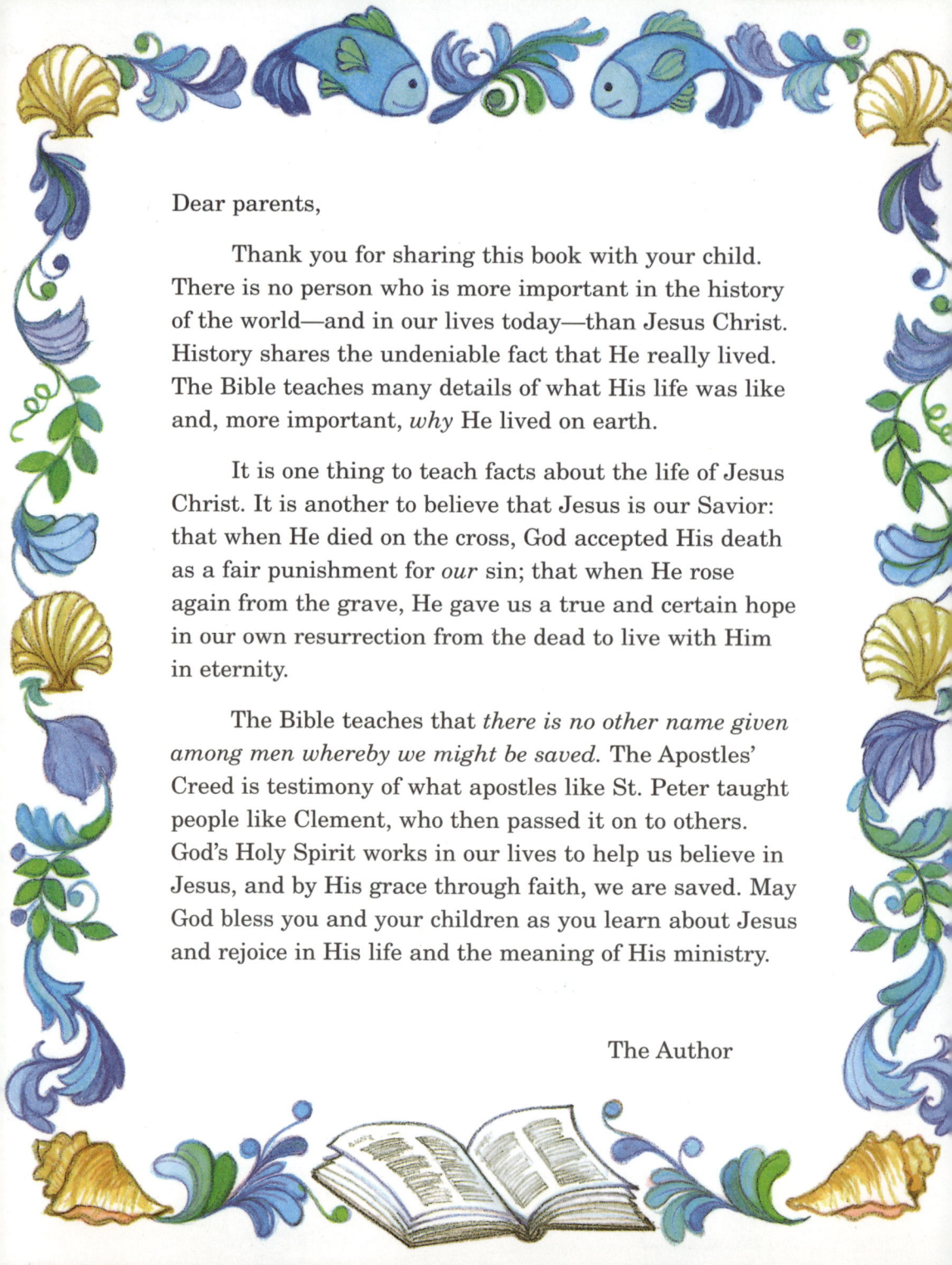

Dear parents,

Thank you for sharing this book with your child. There is no person who is more important in the history of the world—and in our lives today—than Jesus Christ. History shares the undeniable fact that He really lived. The Bible teaches many details of what His life was like and, more important, *why* He lived on earth.

It is one thing to teach facts about the life of Jesus Christ. It is another to believe that Jesus is our Savior: that when He died on the cross, God accepted His death as a fair punishment for *our* sin; that when He rose again from the grave, He gave us a true and certain hope in our own resurrection from the dead to live with Him in eternity.

The Bible teaches that *there is no other name given among men whereby we might be saved.* The Apostles' Creed is testimony of what apostles like St. Peter taught people like Clement, who then passed it on to others. God's Holy Spirit works in our lives to help us believe in Jesus, and by His grace through faith, we are saved. May God bless you and your children as you learn about Jesus and rejoice in His life and the meaning of His ministry.

The Author